Mr Wolf's
Pancakes
Jan Fearnley

With very special
thanks to Genevieve
and Ramona.

First published in Great Britain in 1999 by Mammoth
an imprint of Egmont Children's Books Limited
a division of Egmont Holding Limited
239 Kensington High Street, London W8 6SA
Text and illustrations copyright © Jan Fearnley 1999
Jan Fearnley has asserted her moral rights
A CIP catalogue record for this title is available from the British Library
Printed in Hong Kong

ISBN 0 7497 3559 7

5 7 9 10 8 6

Mr Wolf's
Pancakes
Jan Fearnley

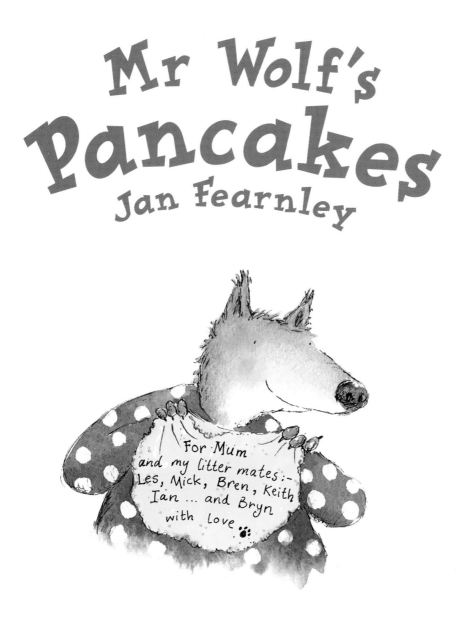

For Mum
and my litter mates:-
Les, Mick, Bren, Keith
Ian ... and Bryn
with love

O ne day, Mr Wolf was feeling hungry.
He fancied some pancakes.
"Yum, yum," he said, licking his lips at the
thought of a big pile of fresh, delicious pancakes.

Mr Wolf had never made pancakes before, so he took his big recipe book down off the shelf and looked inside.

But wolves can't read very well and Mr Wolf had trouble making sense of it. So he went to get some help from his neighbours.

He called on Chicken Licken who lived
next door.

"Please can you help me read this?" he asked.

"No!" said Chicken Licken, slamming the
door in Mr Wolf's face – BANG!

"Oh, dear," sighed Mr Wolf. He sat down, slowly read the book, and worked out what he needed – all by himself.

Mr Wolf looked in his cupboard for the ingredients,
but he couldn't find anything he needed.

"I'll go to the shop," he decided, and he settled down
to write a list.

But wolves aren't very good at writing, so Mr Wolf
called on Wee Willy Winky.

"You're very clever," said Mr Wolf.
"Can you help me write my shopping
list, please?"

"No!" said Wee Willy Winky.
"Go away!" He slammed his door –
BANG!

"There's no need to be like that,"
said Mr Wolf quietly.

Mr Wolf sat down and tried very hard with his writing until he had made his shopping list – all by himself.

Now he needed to count his money to make sure he had enough.

But wolves aren't very good at counting, so he went to the Gingerbread Man for some help.

"Can you help me count my money, please?"
he asked politely.

"No! I'm too busy to bother with you!"
said the Gingerbread Man, slamming his door —
BANG!

So poor Mr Wolf had to sit down and count his money. It took him a long time and he had to check it three times before it was right. But he did it — all by himself.

Mr Wolf needed a basket to carry his shopping, so he called on Little Red Riding Hood.

"Please may I borrow your basket?"
he asked very nicely.

"I'm not lending my basket to you!"
said Little Red Riding Hood. "Now, clear off!"

So Mr Wolf set off to the shop without
a basket.

"I'll manage," he said.

Mr Wolf went to the shop.

He looked at his list, remembered what
he needed, counted out his money, and carried
the eggs, milk and flour home – all by himself.

Now it was time to make the pancakes. But wolves aren't very good at cooking, so Mr Wolf called on the Three Little Pigs.

"Please can you help me cook my pancakes? I'll share them with you," he said kindly.

"No chance!" chorused the pigs, slamming their doors – BANG! BANG! BANG!

Mr Wolf felt sad because nobody wanted to help him.

Mr Wolf went home and started to make the pancakes — all by himself.

Soon there was a huge pile of delicious pancakes on the table, all ready for eating.

Now, as Mr Wolf had been making his pancakes,
a lovely smell had drifted out of the kitchen.

All his neighbours could smell it and it made
them feel very hungry.

They wanted some pancakes too.

They decided to try their luck.

So, they knocked on Mr Wolf's door.

"Give us some of your pancakes!" said the rotten lot.

"Why should I give any to you?" said Mr Wolf. "Not one of you would help me."

"We'll help you eat them," replied Mr Wolf's neighbours nastily. "Anyway, we're not going away until you give us some!"

Mr Wolf thought very hard for a moment.
There was only one decent thing to do.

"Oh, very well then," he sighed, "you had better come in."

Mr Wolf opened the door wide and whoosh!
His greedy neighbours rudely pushed him aside
and dashed down the hall.

Mr Wolf shook his head, shrugged his
shoulders, followed them into the kitchen and
when they were all in . . .

Mr Wolf gobbled them up.

SNIPPITY!

SNAPPITY!

That was the end of his unhelpful neighbours!

And then, with his bulging tummy not quite full,
Mr Wolf sat down to eat his pile of pancakes – and
he did it all by himself.

Well, there was nobody else around.